This edition published in 1995 by Leopard Books,
a division of Random House UK Ltd,
20 Vauxhall Bridge Road, London SW1V 2SA

First published in 1992 by Julia MacRae Books

Text © 1992 Kirsten McKorkell
Illustrations © 1992 Peter Kavanagh

ISBN 0 7529 0154 0

The
Christmas
MOUSE

Kirsten McCorkell
and Peter Kavanagh

LEOPARD

It was Christmas Eve.

Everyone in the family was very busy.
Mum was in the kitchen making her extra-special
large mince pies.

Dad was in the dining room wrapping up
presents. No one was allowed to go in!

Kate and Penny were in the sitting room making the stable for the Nativity Scene.

Millie Mouse was very interested in what they were doing.

Penny had cut up a box and Kate had painted it.

Now they needed some hay to put in the manger
to make a bed for Baby Jesus.

"Let's use some of Millie Mouse's hay,"
said Penny. "I'm sure she won't mind.
Be careful. We don't want Millie to escape . . ."

Too late!
Millie squeezed past Kate's
hand, ran down her arm and disappeared.

Mum and Dad came to help Kate and Penny catch Millie Mouse but it was no good. They couldn't see her,

not the tip of her tail, not even one whisker.
Millie had got clean away! Everyone looked for her.

"Cheer up," said Mum. "Let's put Mary and Joseph into the stable."

"But not Baby Jesus," said Penny. "Baby Jesus won't be born until Christmas Day."

Mum gave Kate and Penny some lemonade and an extra-specially large mince pie to leave on a tray for Father Christmas.

Millie was still missing at bedtime, and Kate and Penny felt very sad. Even the thought of Father Christmas and stockings didn't cheer them up.

B ut on Christmas morning, they rushed downstairs

to see if Father Christmas had eaten his mince pie.

"Oh," cried Penny. "He's eaten nearly all the mince pie. Look at the tiny toothmarks in it."

"Those can't be Father Christmas's nibbly little teeth," said Kate. "He's a big man with big teeth."

"LOOK!" cried Mum.

Mum lifted Millie carefully out of the manger. Millie's whiskers twitched a little but otherwise she didn't stir.

"I think there was too much mince pie for such a little mouse," said Mum.

Then Kate put Baby Jesus in the manger. "Happy Christmas," she said, so softly that only Baby Jesus would hear.